THE 'POSSUM IN THE POOL

Written by: Joy Liebl

Illustrated by: D'Lynn Roll

ISBN: Softcover   978-1-5434-1268-0
        Hardcover   978-1-5434-1269-7
        EBook   978-1-5434-1267-3

Print information available on the last page

Rev. date: 06/12/2017

To order additional copies of this book, contact:
Xlibris
1-888-795-4274
www.Xlibris.com
Orders@Xlibris.com

THE 'POSSUM IN THE POOL

Robby loved to ride on his Mother's back with his brothers and sisters.

Tonight they were heading to a pool surrounded by trees and bushes.

There a kind family left out dishes of cat food for hungry animals to eat.

Robby quickly gobbled up his share of the food and went to explore.

He decided to get closer to the pool and check it out.

"Be very, very careful Robby! If you fall in, I cannot get you out!" said his Mother.

Robby didn't listen! He walked right to the edge of the pool...

AND

    FELL

        IN!

Opossums can swim but Robby knew he was in trouble.

His Mother was frantic!

She had all her other children quickly climb onto her back.

Then she ran around the pool trying to save Robby.

She stuck her paws into the pool hoping to grab him.

She stuck her tail into the pool hoping he could grab onto it.

She even stuck her snout into the pool trying to catch him in her mouth!

Soon Robby was too tired to swim anymore.

He found a tiny ledge to sit on where he could just keep his nose above water.

Robby's Mother told him that they would have to wait for the humans to find him and save him in the morning.

She crawled under some bushes very close to Robby and talked to him the whole night long so that he would not be so alone and afraid.

Robby was hoping that these humans woke up early because he was very cold and tired.

Fortunately they did get up early to feed the birds and to put out more of the good cat food for the animals.

As the kind woman walked past the pool she spotted poor Robby...

BUBBLES COMING OUT OF HIS NOSE!

"Oh my!" she exclaimed and quickly called her husband to come and help.

He took the long handled pool net and held it up to Robby's front paws.

Robby grabbed on and they lifted him up and out of the pool to safety.

Robby was placed gently on the ground, soaking wet from head to tail.

Plus, his nose was full of water!

CHOO!

Robby shook the water off of one back leg and then the other.

Then he gave a big 'possum smile to the two kind humans.

He found his Mother close by and quickly crawled up on her back.

He snuggled in amongst his brothers and sisters to get dry and warm.

His Mother was very, very happy to have him safe.

But, every day his Mother reminded him to stay away from pools.

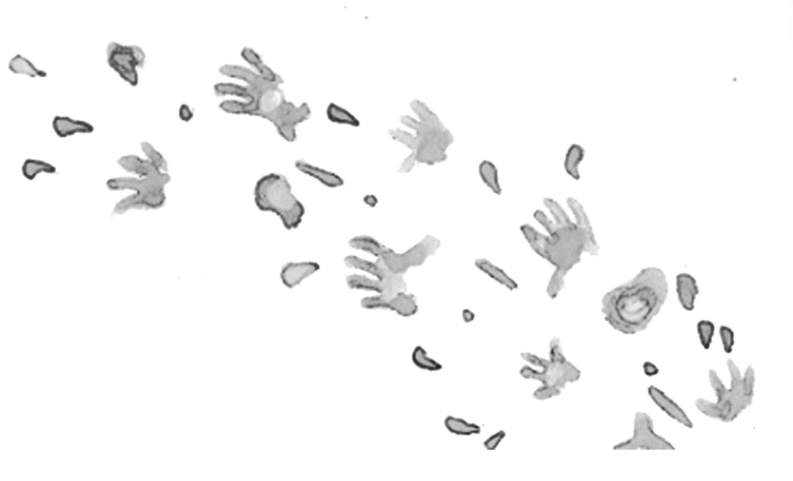

And, of course, he did!